MCR

P9-DEZ-734

JPicture
Jsarf. E

For my Ruth

The illustrations in this book were drawn digitally
and painted in Photoshop.

Cataloging-in-Publication Data has been applied for and may be obtained
from the Library of Congress.

ISBN 978-1-4197-3168-6

Text and illustrations copyright © 2017 Einat Tsarfati
Text translated from the original Hebrew by Annette Appel
Book design by Julia Marvel

This edition published in 2019 by Abrams Books for Young Readers, an
imprint of ABRAMS. All rights reserved. No portion of this book may
be reproduced, stored in a retrieval system, or transmitted in any form
or by any means, mechanical, electronic, photocopying, recording, or
otherwise, without written permission from the publisher.

Printed and bound in China
10 9 8 7 6 5 4 3 2 1

Abrams Books for Young Readers are available at special discounts
when purchased in quantity for premiums and promotions as well as
fundraising or educational use. Special editions can also be created to
specification. For details, contact specialsales@abramsbooks.com or the
address below.

 ABRAMS The Art of Books
195 Broadway, New York, NY 10007
abramsbooks.com

THE NEIGHBORS

EVANSTON PUBLIC LIBRARY

1703 ORRINGTON AVENUE

EVANSTON, ILLINOIS 60201

EINAT TSARFATI

Translated from Hebrew by Annette Appel

ABRAMS BOOKS FOR YOUNG READERS | NEW YORK

I live in a building that is seven stories high.

Every floor has a slightly different door.

The first door has a lot of locks.

That apartment belongs to a family of thieves.
They just love ancient Egyptian artifacts.

The second door is always surrounded by muddy footprints.

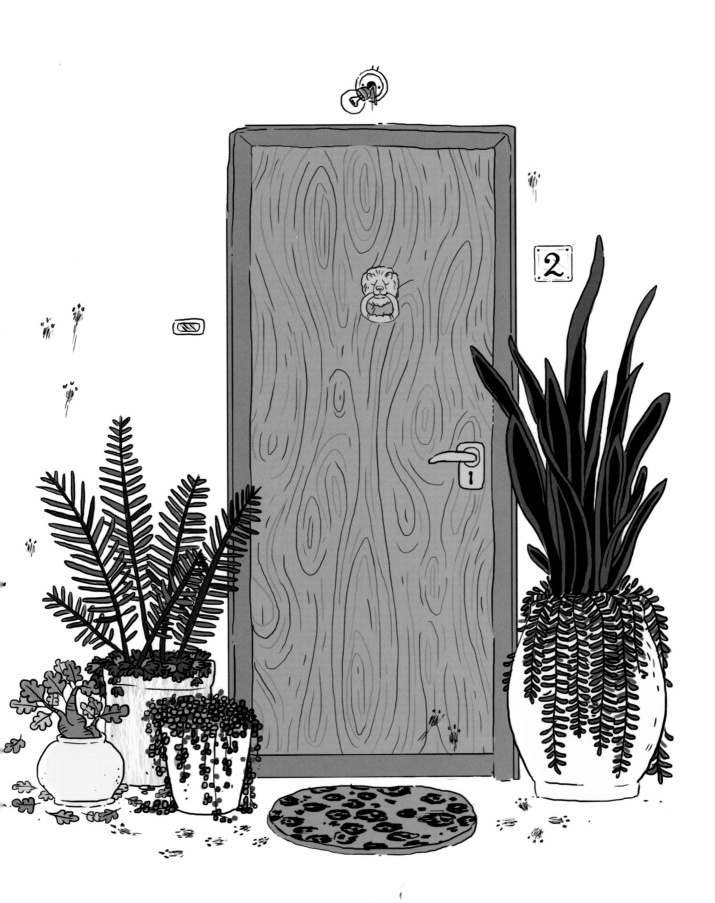

That is the home of an old explorer and his pet tiger.

The red door is the door with the wheel.

Behind that door lives a family of acrobats. They are always looking for ways to improve their act.

When I reach the fourth door,
the light always shuts off . . .

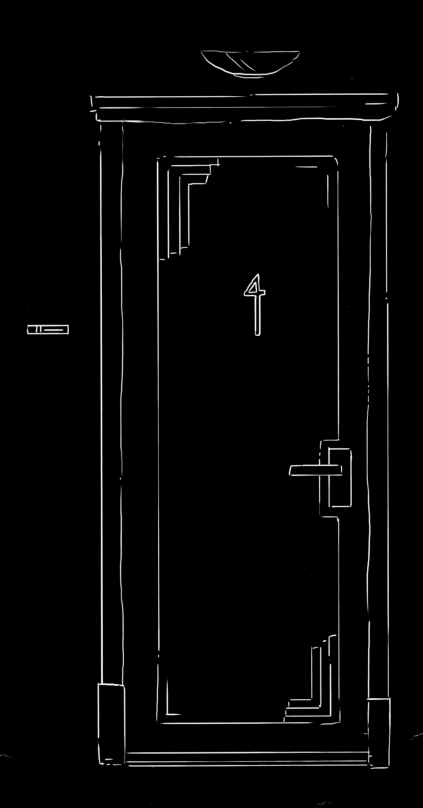

. . . because that is the vampire's apartment.

The fifth door smells like pickled fish.

Inside, the pirate lives with his love.

I always stop at the sixth door to listen to really cool music that flows out into the hall.

The musical family who lives inside celebrates someone's birthday at least once a week.

The seventh door is where I live with my parents.

They are so boring.

But I love them . . .

. . . and they love me.